0500000457472 4

D0097968

ER Mar
Marcia
Bemelr
Madel:

DEC 1 9 2012

Dear Parents and Educators,

Welcome to Penguin Young Readers! As parents and educators, you know that each child develops at his or her own pace—in terms of speech, critical thinking, and, of course, reading. Penguin Young Readers recognizes this fact. As a result, each Penguin Young Readers book is assigned a traditional easy-to-read level (1–4) as well as a Guided Reading Level (A–P). Both of these systems will help you choose the right book for your child. Please refer to the back of each book for specific leveling information. Penguin Young Readers features esteemed authors and illustrators, stories about favorite characters, fascinating nonfiction, and more!

Madeline's Tea Party

LEVEL 2

GUIDED READING LEVEL **I**

This book is perfect for a **Progressing Reader** who:
- can figure out unknown words by using picture and context clues;
- can recognize beginning, middle, and ending sounds;
- can make and confirm predictions about what will happen in the text; and
- can distinguish between fiction and nonfiction.

Here are some **activities** you can do during and after reading this book:
- Character Traits: Come up with a list of words to describe Pepito. How did his character change at the end of the story?
- Vocabulary: Some of the words in this book may be unfamiliar. Find each of the words below in the text. Do you know the definition? Can you use picture or text clues to figure out the meaning? Look up the definitions of the words below in the dictionary and any other words you do not understand.

gloom	proper	smartly
hosting	selfish	strolls

Remember, sharing the love of reading with a child is the best gift you can give!

—Bonnie Bader, EdM
   Penguin Young Readers program

*Penguin Young Readers are leveled by independent reviewers applying the standards developed by Irene Fountas and Gay Su Pinnell in *Matching Books to Readers: Using Leveled Books in Guided Reading*, Heinemann, 1999.

Penguin Young Readers
Published by the Penguin Group
Penguin Group (USA) Inc., 375 Hudson Street, New York, New York 10014, USA
Penguin Group (Canada), 90 Eglinton Avenue East, Suite 700, Toronto, Ontario M4P 2Y3, Canada
(a division of Pearson Penguin Canada Inc.)
Penguin Books Ltd., 80 Strand, London WC2R 0RL, England
Penguin Group Ireland, 25 St. Stephen's Green, Dublin 2, Ireland (a division of Penguin Books Ltd.)
Penguin Group (Australia), 250 Camberwell Road, Camberwell, Victoria 3124, Australia
(a division of Pearson Australia Group Pty. Ltd.)
Penguin Books India Pvt. Ltd., 11 Community Centre, Panchsheel Park, New Delhi—110 017, India
Penguin Group (NZ), 67 Apollo Drive, Rosedale, Auckland 0632, New Zealand
(a division of Pearson New Zealand Ltd.)
Penguin Books (South Africa) (Pty.) Ltd., 24 Sturdee Avenue,
Rosebank, Johannesburg 2196, South Africa

Penguin Books Ltd., Registered Offices: 80 Strand, London WC2R 0RL, England

Text and illustrations copyright © 2012 by John Bemelmans Marciano. Character of Madeline © 2012 by
Ludwig Bemelmans, LLC. All rights reserved. Published in 2012 by Penguin Young Readers, an imprint
of Penguin Group (USA) Inc., 345 Hudson Street, New York, New York 10014. Printed in the U.S.A.

Library of Congress Cataloging-in-Publication Data is available.

ISBN 978-0-448-45439-9 (pbk)   10 9 8 7 6 5 4 3 2 1
ISBN 978-0-448-45735-2 (hc)   10 9 8 7 6 5 4 3 2 1

MADELINE'S
TEA PARTY

written by John Bemelmans Marciano
illustrated by JT Morrow
based on the art of John Bemelmans Marciano

Penguin Young Readers
An Imprint of Penguin Group (USA) Inc.

In an old house in Paris

that is covered with vines,

live twelve little girls

in two straight lines.

They leave the house

at half past nine.

The smallest one is Madeline.

Madeline is hosting

an afternoon tea.

The party begins at half past three.

The girls come in

all smartly dressed.

Each one wears her Sunday best.

One last guest is very late.

The girls must sit and wait

and wait.

At last, at almost half past four,

a most selfish boy strolls

through the door.

He won't say he's sorry

or take off his hat.

But that is Pepito,

the world's greatest brat.

Madeline fills each cup with tea.

The girls drink it up

most happily.

Pepito takes a sip.

He makes a face.

He spits out tea

all over the place.

"This party stinks!" he says.

"But you know what's fun?

Magic tricks—I'll show you one!"

"Watch how

the amazing Pepito is able

to remove the cloth out

from this table!"

But his magic skills are fake!

The cups all fly around

and break.

The bad hat laughs.

The girls are sad.

Now Madeline is really mad.

"If you can't behave in

a proper way,

please, Pepito, GO AWAY!"

"Fine!" he says.

"I don't want to stay.

It's a silly party, anyway!"

He starts to leave

but in comes a cake.

Maybe Pepito made a mistake!

The cake is a surprise

from Madeline's father.

The girls all cheer

and hug each other.

As the cake is cut,

the boy's heart sinks.

"I should have been nicer,"

Pepito thinks.

He is followed home

by a cloud of gloom.

Now Pepito cries

alone in his room.

Then he hears the *bing-bang-bong*

of the doorbell's mighty gong.

He sees Madeline at the door.

But what has *she* come here for?

"There was an extra slice of cake

I thought that you might like to take."

Pepito looks up, down,

and all around.

He kicks a rock lying

on the ground.

He says, "I'm sorry

for how I behaved before.

I promise not to be

such a brat anymore."

31

Pepito thanks Madeline

for the lovely treat.

And the two good friends

sit down to eat.